Colleen Alexander.

Aug 24 / 2023

Work Shop !

WELCOME
TO THE
CYPHER

WORDS BY
KHODI DILL

PICTURES BY
AWURADWOA AFFUL

annick
press
toronto · berkeley

Follow my finger snaps.
Follow the beatbox and
follow the claps.

Come on inside
the cypher.

I wanna show you how to rap.
Imagine that.

Imagine all the words.
Imagine how they curve
over the **boom-bap!**
Can you vibe with that?

Are you ready to begin?
Can you dive into the groove
while the record player spins?

You wanna ride with the rappers
who are gathered in the round?

Together
we can lift each other
right off the ground!

You'll see, li'l one.

So tell me,
are you down?

Say word. Come on, yo!
Lemme show you how we flow
over rapids on the river of music.
Imagine, though!

Imagine all the ways
to ride a sound wave.
See how a word plays?

You can turn a simple phrase
into imagery that soars
and emotions that **roar!**
Into a fire that warms us
right down to the core.

And you can let your fire out
in a whisper or a **shout!**
All feelings are welcome in the cypher,
no doubt.

So if you yearn to ignite,
then let your words **burn bright!**

Watch them twist
and see them turn.
Watch them teach.
You will learn!

See, rap is a style that is infinitely free.
All you need is a beat
and your **soul's poetry.**

And an ear to tune in
to that cool ruckus raised
and the magician making words
come alive in new ways.

Just imagine all the freedom.
Imagine all the buzz

on a beatboxer's lips
as she does what she does.

To break open the silence
in a place where it's quiet,
**inciting an exciting
and musical riot!**

C'mon, li'l one!
See what you can do!
See how it feels
when your words **ring true.**

Righteous like the rhythm
of a raised boom box
birthing a new movement
from the streets of the Bronx.

Feel its bass **booming**
right down to your feet,
and embrace the true meaning
of freedom of speech.

Come and let it all out.
Your pride and your fear
and your love . . .
and your **clout!**

That's that **heat**, li'l one.
**That's what I'm
talkin' about!**

Welcome to the cypher!
Now huddle up nice and snug.
You feel that circle around you?
Well, that's a **hip-hop hug!**

Come close and feel the warmth and the music within.
Feel the zone that you enter when you really **go in**.

It's a home for your **voice** and your **heart and your spirit.**

So open your mouth and **let everyone hear it!**

Say, "I'm an ever-eager truth speaker,
a rhythm-seekin' rhyme weaver.
I'm an ever-present off-the-top
and effervescent **fire breather!**"

That's it, li'l one.
C'mon now, gimme daps!
Just like that, you can rap.
You can rap!

When you're in the cypher circle,
unbroken and true,
you will marvel as your own poems
surprise even you!

So tell 'em,
"This is a voice
that represents me!"

And feel the greatest
feeling that ever could be:
that art from the heart
of a **brand-new**
emcee!

Wow, li'l one!
I bet you had a li'l fun.

And I hope you **never stop**
now that you've begun

making bars bounce off beats
and making puns touch the sun.
Taking music to the streets
while the record player spun

and skated

and scratched.

You see, sometimes revolution
wears a backwards cap
and is waged in **finger snaps**
and **fist bumps** and **claps.**

So take a turn in the cypher,
that **great circle of rap,**
spanning every street corner,
every inch of the map.

Bodies movin', heads bobbin'
while a beauty beat drops.
Above all, **a great storm cloud
of musical thoughts.**

See, in the cypher, li'l one,
everyone is welcome.
In the cypher,
even **you** can become an emcee.

And **powerful**
and **equal**
and **infinite**
and **free.**

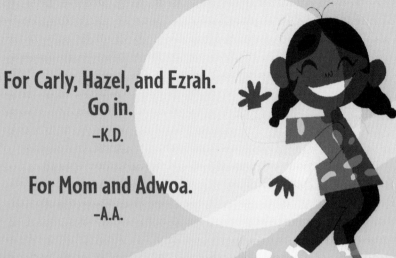

For Carly, Hazel, and Ezrah.
Go in.
–K.D.

For Mom and Adwoa.
–A.A.

KHODI DILL is a Bahamian-Canadian writer of everything from rap songs to children's literature. He is a practicing anti-racist educator with a passion for social justice and the arts. Khodi is a proud father and partner who lives and writes in Saskatoon, Saskatchewan.

AWURADWOA AFFUL is a Ghanaian-Canadian designer, illustrator, and animator. She was born and raised in Toronto, Ontario.

© 2021 Khodi Dill (text)
© 2021 Awuradwoa Afful (illustrations)
Second printing, August 2022

Cover art by Awuradwoa Afful, designed by Paul Covello
Interior designed by Paul Covello
Edited by Claire Caldwell

Annick Press Ltd.

We acknowledge the support of the Canada Council for the Arts and the Ontario Arts Council, and the participation of the Government of Canada/la participation du gouvernement du Canada for our publishing activities.

ONTARIO ARTS COUNCIL
CONSEIL DES ARTS DE L'ONTARIO
an Ontario government agency
un organisme du gouvernement de l'Ontario

Library and Archives Canada Cataloguing in Publication

Title: Welcome to the cypher / words by Khodi Dill ; pictures by Awuradwoa Afful.
Names: Dill, Khodi, author. | Afful, Awuradwoa, illustrator.
Identifiers: Canadiana (print) 20210189363 | Canadiana (ebook) 2021018938X | ISBN 9781773215631 (hardcover) | ISBN 9781773215662 (PDF) | ISBN 9781773215655 (HTML)
Subjects: LCGFT: Picture books.
Classification: LCC PS8607.I457 W45 2021 | DDC jC813/.6–dc23

Published in the U.S.A. by Annick Press (U.S.) Ltd.
Distributed in Canada by University of Toronto Press.
Distributed in the U.S.A. by Publishers Group West.

Printed in China

annickpress.com
thegreygriot.com
awuradwoa-afful.com

Also available as an e-book. Please visit annickpress.com/ebooks for more details.